GULF GATE LIBRARY
7112 CURTISS AVENUE
SARASOTA, FL 34231

JUN 2 6 2011

A Puppy for the
White House

GULF GATE LIBRARY
7112 CURTISS AVENUE
SARASOTA, FL 34231.

Kathleen Smith

Illustrations by Laurie Hansen

Lollipop Publishing, LLC
Westminster, CO

3 1969 02079 5661

text © 2009 Kathleen Smith
illustrations © 2009 Laurie Hansen

All rights reserved. No part of this book may be reproduced or transmitted in any form or by any means, electronic or mechanical, including photocopying, recording, or by any information storage and retrieval system, without permission in writing from the publisher.

Published by
Lollipop Publishing, LLC
Westminster, CO

Publisher's Cataloging-in-Publication Data
Smith, Kathleen.

    A puppy for the White House / written by Kathleen Smith ; illustrated
by Laurie Hansen. – Westminster, CO : Lollipop Pub., LLC, 2009.

    p. ; cm.

    Summary: Ms. Smith's classroom writes a story about the first family's quest to find a puppy in hopes of winning a class contest.

    ISBN: 978-0-615-30165-5

    1. Presidents' pets--United States--Juvenile fiction. 2. Children of presidents--United States--Juvenile fiction. 3. Obama, Barack--Family--Juvenile fiction. 4. White House (Washington, D.C.)--Juvenile fiction. 5. Puppies--Juvenile fiction. I. Hansen, Laurie. II. Title.

E176.48.S65 2009
[E]—dc22   2009930440

Project coordination by Jenkins Group, Inc.
www.BookPublishing.com

Graphic design by Creative Illustrations & Designs

Printed in the United States of America
13 12 11 10 09 • 5 4 3 2 1

While most of this book is realistic fiction some of the quotes were actual words spoken by Mr. Obama during various speeches, commercials, and interviews both during his campaign and after his election and are considered public domain.

Dedicated to everyone who has
waited for their first puppy.

On the chalkboard:
Bb Cc Dd Ee

* FIELD T[...]
THURSD[...]
- Bring [...]
- Permiss[...]

After the Pledge of Allegiance Ms. Smith stood before the class and asked, "How many of you watched the presidential election last night?" Their hands flew in the air like the American flag, patriotic and proud. She continued, "Did any of you get to watch the acceptance speech in Grant Park?"

Jennifer raised her hand, but before she was called on, blurted out, "Yes! Did you hear what he said to his daughters? He said, 'Sasha and Malia, I love you both more than you can imagine. And you have earned the new puppy that is coming with us to the White House.'"

"Jennifer, you must have read my mind. While I watched the speech last night, I was excited for those girls. Let's all imagine the car ride home. The girls must have

been thrilled. Now for your next assignment, I want you to make up the conversation they had in the car about puppies. Be sure to give each member of the family a chance to share his or her thoughts. And because you will be writing about real people, you will need to respect their privacy and use pronouns instead of their real names. So, let's get out our writing books and begin writing."

The timer was set. Ten minutes later, Ms. Smith said, "Class, put down your pencils. Does anyone care to share what they have written?"

Juanita raised her hand.

"Let's begin with you, Juanita."

She picked up her paper and began reading… "The older child exclaimed, 'I'm so excited! I want a Goldendoodle.'"

"That was excellent,

Juanita. Just what I was looking for." Then addressing the class, she continued, "We are not stopping here, class. This is your long-term homework assignment. I want each of you to write a realistic story about the First Family adopting their dog, starting from the first words said by President Obama to his kids until the actual date that they take the puppy home to the White House. There is a national writing contest our class will be entering. Using parts from each of your stories we'll create our class masterpiece. To help everyone remain focused and realistic, we'll keep a list of events that have happened on the campaign trail, on election night or things that you've heard on the news that have to do with the selection of their puppy. Be sure to include some traditional family values in your story; for example, love for one another, respect, and the value of an education. Now put away your writing book and take out your math books. Please turn to page 119."

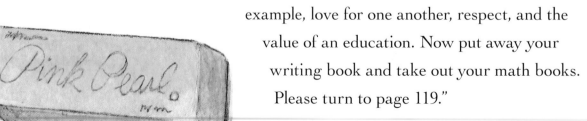

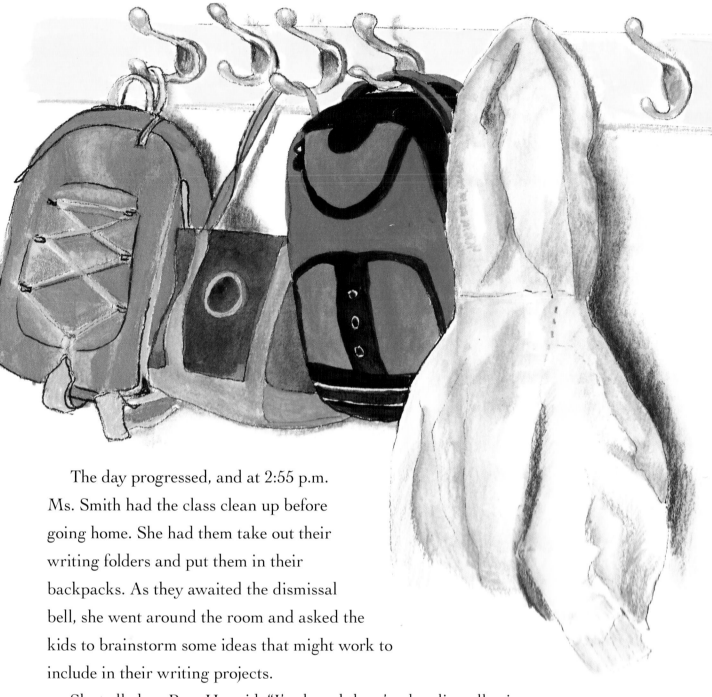

The day progressed, and at 2:55 p.m. Ms. Smith had the class clean up before going home. She had them take out their writing folders and put them in their backpacks. As they awaited the dismissal bell, she went around the room and asked the kids to brainstorm some ideas that might work to include in their writing projects.

She called on Ben. He said, "I've heard there's a bowling alley in the White House. What if we include that in our story? Because we've all heard about how the President bowled on the campaign trail."

"Perfect," Ms. Smith proclaimed with a smile, and she began writing it on the big chart paper in the front of the room. She continued, "Class, I want you to become super sleuths and ferret out any news that has to do with the First Family or the First Puppy. Each morning we will begin our day writing on this chart." The final bell rang.

Ms. Smith finished, "Have a good night and I will see you tomorrow. Class dismissed."

After months of hard work and many revisions, the class story was finally
finished. The students were filled with anticipation as they gathered on the rug.
As soon as they were seated and had settled down, Ms. Smith opened the book
and began reading.

In Search of the Perfect Puppy

?

?

?

By Ms. Smith's fifth grade class

His daughters were standing on the stage in Grant Park when they heard his heart-felt words. "I love you both more than you can imagine and you have earned the new puppy that is coming with us to the White House."

"A puppy!" they exclaimed as they drove back to their home.

"I am so excited! I want a Goldendoodle!" the older girl cried.

"Honey, before we decide we need to look at all the breeds and find one that is hypoallergenic for your allergies," her mother insisted.

"A Puggle has short hair," the younger one pointed out.

Their father added, "Nothing too girlie. I'd like to find a shelter dog, but obviously most of those dogs are mutts like me."

They arrived home.
Their mother stated,
"It's been a long, long day, so
time for bed, you two. We can begin
our search tomorrow," as she kissed them
each good night.

They ran to kiss their father. Both children hugged
him close.

His older daughter beamed, "I'm so proud of you, Dad."

His younger daughter chimed in, "You'll make a great,
great president."

Then they both exclaimed, "We love you very much!"

He kissed them each goodnight and said, "Sweet dreams.
I love you both."

38

The next
morning the older
child brought a book about dog
breeds to the kitchen table. She opened the book and began flipping through the
pages. Her sister sidled up to her so she could see as well.

Their mother brought the food to the table. "Girls, put the book away for now.
You know the rule: no books while we are eating."

Her daughter flipped one more page, then caught her mother's stern look. She
closed the book, put it on the counter, and returned to her place at the table and
began eating her pancakes.

"Mom," she began, "do you think after breakfast we could go to the library and
get some more books on dogs?"

"I have already let you sleep in. Even though you are late, you will be going to school today. I promise to have all the information we will need when you get home."

The daughter was about to plead her case to stay home, but before she could begin, however, her father said, "You know my views on the value of an education. My mother instilled in me its importance. 'She'd wake me up at 4:30 in the morning, and we'd sit there and go through my lessons. And I used to complain and grumble. And she'd say, well this is no picnic for me either, buster.' But as much as I grumbled, I learned that an education is the ticket to success. So, I don't want to hear any more talk about missing school. You do well in your classes today, and your mother will be doing her homework as well, and she will be ready when you come home."

The girls loved the university's lab school usually, but today their minds were busy thinking of puppies. A few times during the day they were caught daydreaming. Their teachers attributed it to the fact that their father was elected President of the United States.

Finally the last bell rang and school was dismissed. As the older girl walked out of class her English teacher stopped her and said, "Get some rest tonight you weren't yourself today. And please tell your father congratulations."

"Thanks, I'll tell him."

The girls found each other and hurried to the bus. They climbed aboard. Ms. Elisa greeted them with a smile. "Well, girls, it looks like you two will be getting a puppy."

"We're going to do some research to find one that won't bother my sister's allergies," related the younger girl.

Ms. Elisa volunteered, "I have a Yorkie-poo. It doesn't shed and it makes a great companion."

"Thank you, Ms. Elisa."

At their stop the girls thanked Ms. Elisa again and hurried off the bus. Their mother was waiting for them.

Oo Pp Qq Rr Ss Tt Uu Vv Ww Xx Yy Zz

"Mom," the girls called out. They ran to her and hugged her tight.

"Did you do your homework?" the younger daughter asked.

"Of course," her mother replied.

They climbed the steps to their house. Usually the girls went to the kitchen for their afternoon snack but today they headed toward the office where their computer was kept.

Their mother said, "Girls, come to the kitchen I have your snack ready, and all the information is spread out on the table."

They raced down the hall to the kitchen, fueled with excitement. Usually their mother would scold them for running in the house, but today she ignored it and hurried after them.

They both sat at the table and looked at all the papers scattered there. "Both of you come over to the counter to have your milk and cookies."

"Mom, we've waited all day," the younger one complained.

"More like almost two years," the older one corrected her.

"Well then, you both are used to waiting so you can wait a few more minutes. The cookies are freshly baked. Your favorite: chocolate chip."

"Thanks, Mom," said the oldest daughter. "You're the best! Can you tell us what you found out while we eat?"

"Sure," their mother answered, "I went to an Internet site that listed all the dogs that would be less aggravating to your allergies. I learned, however, that there is really no hypoallergenic dog. But we can look for certain things."

"Let's make up our own breed. How 'bout a Schnauziepoo?" the younger one offered.

"That's a Schnoodle," snickered the older girl. "But if we mixed a West Highland Terrier with a Blue Heeler, we could make a Blue High Heeler."

"We could dress it up in pearls and a velvet hat," the younger one carried on. But then she remembered her father's words... Nothing too girlie and stopped herself before her imagination ignited.

"What about a Boxerpoo?" their mother interjected.

The girls giggled hysterically at that one.

"Is there something funny about a Boxer/Poodle mix?" their mother inquired with feigned seriousness.

The girls looked at each other and then broke into fresh rounds of hysterical laughter.

Their father walked in. "What's so funny?"

The older daughter replied, "We were just thinking of new breeds and Mom said we should get a Boxapoo!"

They all laughed.

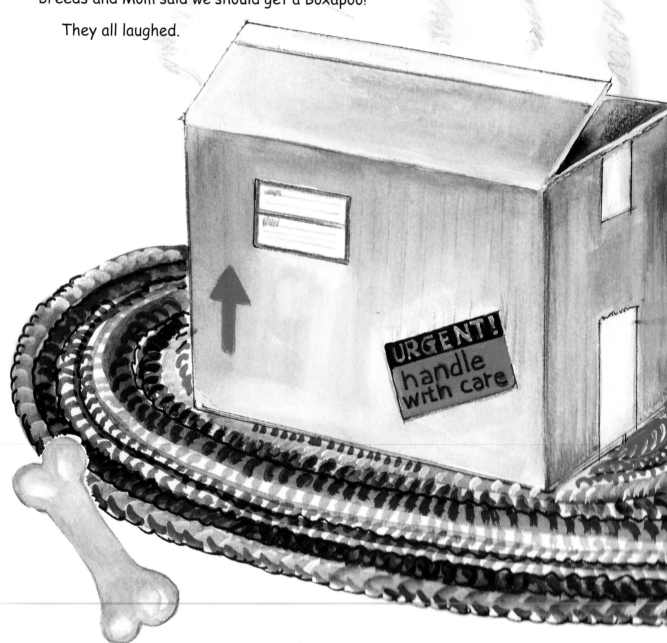

Father said, "Well, I did get an offer from the Friends of the Peruvian Hairless Dog Association. They want to give you girls a four-month-old pedigreed male puppy. They have named it Ears. I thanked them for their gracious offer but explained to them that this will be a personal family decision. But, if we did get that one, we could change its name to Machu Picchu."

"Oh, Dad, that's funny," the girls laughed.

"Girls do you have any homework?"

"No," they both rejoiced.

"Well," their father said, "take these papers to your room and finish looking them over."

Mother stopped them and said, "Before you go, I forgot to tell you my news. The First Lady called me today and told me something that I know will make you both very happy."

"Tell us, please!" both girls begged.

"Well, there is a bowling alley in the White House. Now your dad can practice anytime he wants!" Everyone laughed because they knew how he had bowled in Pennsylvania on the campaign trail.

"Is that what you were going to tell us?" the older child asked.

"No, I was going to tell you that she told me about a secret garden where you can walk and play with the puppy, and it's completely hidden from view."

"Wow, just like the book *The Secret Garden* by Frances Hodgson Burnett. That was one of our favorite books, Mom. Just think... a secret garden," the older daughter mused.

The girls picked up all the papers and hurried to their room.

Three hours later the mother called the girls for dinner. "Homemade spaghetti, our favorite!" the girls shouted as they entered the room.

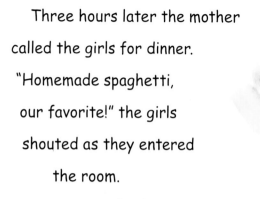

"Help set the table, girls." When they were seated they all held hands and said grace, as was their tradition. Father said, "Girls, I know the promise I made to you last night, but in fairness to all of us, especially the puppy, your mother and I think we should wait until we are settled into the White House. I think we can begin the hunt for our puppy in the spring."

The sisters gave each other a look of pure exasperation. They knew they couldn't try cajoling their parents, and their frustration showed. Mother looked at the girls and said, "Girls, I know you are disappointed, but just think the big adjustment it will be to live in the White House, and until we know our way around, we cannot add a puppy. It would be just too stressful."

The older one looked at her little sister and admitted, "You know they're right. This will really give us a chance to find the best puppy for all of us."

Father looked at his daughter with new eyes and said, "That was a very grown up response. I am proud of you. Don't worry, though; the time will pass quickly enough."

The younger one piped in, "I agree with Sis. Are you proud of me too?"

Both parents smiled lovingly at the children and then their father affirmed, "Yes, we are so proud of both of you."

Time had passed quickly. In Washington, D.C., the girls had made new friends and were enjoying their new school very much. Their father had been sworn in and was now the 44th President of the United States of America.

The girls were thrilled to finally be living in the White House. One evening at dinner they asked again about getting the puppy. But the response was the same... "No, not yet."

Spring arrived and the secret garden came to life. The girls enjoyed sitting out in it, hidden from view. The only person they did see was the White House gardener who was forever busy pulling weeds, pruning, and manicuring the pristine garden.

One day he asked what kind of puppy they had decided on. The older girl said, "A Labradoodle or a Portuguese Water Dog!"

"Oh, so you've narrowed the choices down to two, huh? I've heard you have really spent some time figuring out what kind of breed you want."

The younger girl said, "Dad has told people that he's had more trouble picking a dog than a Commerce Secretary."

The gardener chuckled and said, "It is good to do your homework. A dog is a big commitment; it's smart to spend the time selecting the perfect puppy for your family."

In April, as promised, a perfect puppy did join the family, a second-chance Portie named Bo.

The End.

The class
sat in silence. Ms. Smith
asked, "What do you think?
Do you like it?"

The class began clapping and
shouted, "We love it!"

Ms. Smith beamed, "You have all
become great authors!"

Kelly raised her hand and
questioned, "If they choose our book
and we win, will we be on TV?"

Ms. Smith replied, with a
twinkle in her eye, "Yes, I believe
we will."

With that, the class erupted with
cheers and laughter, the teacher's
words fanning the wildfires of
their imagination.

About the Author

Kathleen Smith is a retired schoolteacher who lives in Westminster, Colorado, with her two dogs, Daisy and Amos. When asked what she was going to do after her retirement she stated: clean the basement and closets in her house. It is her sixth year of retirement and the closets and basement still need cleaning. Instead, she fills her time taking long walks, reading good books, and spending time with her family and friends.

About the Illustrator

For over twelve years, artist Laurie Hansen has painted murals and other commissioned artwork throughout northern Colorado. Her style is as unique and varied as the people she paints for. She and her husband, Steve, live in Thornton, Colorado with their sons, Joel and Kyle.

About the Dog

Bo is a Portuguese Water Dog that was a gift from Senator Ted Kennedy of Massachusetts. The girls named him Bo because their cousins have a cat named Bo and their grandfather was nicknamed Diddley. He was six months old when he moved into the White House.